THE RIVER DRAGON

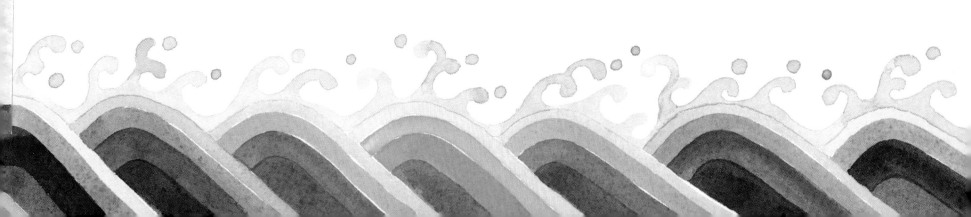

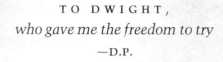

TO DWIGHT,
who gave me the freedom to try
—D.P.

TO MY FATHER,
who opened the door of art for me
—J.T.

CHINESE DRAGONS are traditionally portrayed with very specific characteristics: the head of a camel, horns of a deer, eyes of a demon, ears of an ox, neck of a snake, scales of a carp, palms of a tiger, and claws of a hawk. Beings of great power, they control the thunder and lightning and live in the heavens and under the waters of the earth. They fly without wings, usually surrounded by clouds or mist, and are frequently shown clutching a great pearl in their claws or jaws. Passionately fond of swallows, they have a keen sense of smell and are afraid only of centipedes and five-colored silk scarves.

The illustrations for this book are not set in any one period of Chinese history. Instead, the details of costume and setting are drawn from several different eras to create a believable and timeless world. The paintings were done in watercolor and ink on Arches paper.

First Edition   1   2   3   4   5   6   7   8   9   10

Library of Congress Cataloging in Publication Data
Pattison, Darcy S. The river dragon / by Darcy S. Pattison ; illustrated by Jean and Mou-sien Tseng.
p.   cm. Summary: Ying Shao must make three dangerous trips across the river dragon's bridge before he can marry the lovely Kai-Li.   ISBN 0-688-10426-6.—ISBN 0-688-10427-4 (library)   [1. Dragons—Fiction.]   I. Tseng, Jean, ill.   II. Tseng, Mou-sien, ill.   III. Title.
PZ7.P27816Ri   1991   [Fic]—dc20   90-49931   CIP   AC

THE
RIVER
DRAGON

DARCY PATTISON

ILLUSTRATED BY
JEAN AND MOU-SIEN TSENG

LOTHROP, LEE & SHEPARD BOOKS • NEW YORK

Once there were dragons in the land near the Jasper River. They hatched out of large river pebbles and leaped into the sky with a roar. They ruled over the clouds and rivers and seas and oceans.

Ying Shao, a humble blacksmith, lived and worked on the banks of the Jasper River. He toiled at his forges and never troubled with the dragons except to thank them for the rains.

Ying Shao had been betrothed in childhood to the third daughter of his father's friend, a goldsmith. But since Ying Shao had chosen the profession of blacksmithing, the goldsmith was displeased. He had delayed the wedding, but at long last a date had been set. Kal-Li, the bride-to-be, invited Ying Shao to three banquets before the wedding, as was the custom of their people.

On the day of the first banquet, Ying Shao set out at dusk for the goldsmith's house. He had to travel over

the Jasper River and through the valley. As he stepped onto the bridge, he bowed and set a bowl of rice in the center of the cobblestone road.

"Honorable River Dragon, I thank you for safe passage across your bridge and offer you this bowl of rice as a token of my esteem."

Then he bowed again. He always waited, expecting an answer. No answer ever came, but the bowl was always gone on his return.

The goldsmith gave a splendid banquet. But Ying Shao barely saw anything except Kal-Li. He was fascinated by her jade-fine fingers lifting tidbits to her mouth.

Course followed course of rich foods until the servants brought in the main dish: swallows in delicate curry sauce.

Ying Shao looked at the swallows on his plate in dismay. He had to cross over the River Dragon's bridge on his way home. Everyone knew that dragons love swallows more than anything else. With swallows in his belly, the dragon was sure to eat him.

The goldsmith smiled slyly and said, "Eat. Curried swallows are a special recipe of Kal-Li's mother."

Under the watchful eyes of the parents, Ying Shao ate all the swallows on his plate.

At the end of the meal, a servant brought each guest a fortune cookie. Ying Shao opened his fortune and read:

River Dragon's greatest love:
"Give me swallows," he says with greed.
River Dragon's greatest fear:
"Keep away the centipede."

Ying Shao's heart leaped. Now he knew how to get over the Jasper River. He just had to find a centipede. It was true that they were scarce during fall, but surely he could find just one.

After the party ended, Ying Shao started for home. He watched carefully for signs of a centipede, for his life depended on finding one. The closer he came to the river, the more he worried.

Finally the bridge was in sight. He heard a roar, like a tumbling waterfall. The River Dragon smelled the swallows in his belly!

Then, right before him on the road, Ying Shao saw a large centipede. Its legs rippled as it walked. Ying Shao carefully plucked it out of the dust and put it into his leather pouch.

Now he boldly marched up to the bridge. As his foot touched it, Ti Lung, the River Dragon, flew up and landed in front of him.

Ti Lung dipped his horned head and shook his whiskers. His tail waved from side to side. *Clish*, *clash*, the mighty spikes clanged on the cobblestones. In one back claw the dragon clutched the largest pearl Ying Shao had ever seen.

"Honorable Sir," said Ti Lung in a voice like the clink of copper coins. "I smell swallows. No doubt you realize that I have tired of your meager offerings of rice and have brought me a more worthy gift. Where are the swallows? Give them to me," he demanded.

"Of course, Honorable Ti Lung."

Ying Shao reached into his pouch and pulled out the centipede. He threw it in the River Dragon's face.

"Hsi! Hsi!" roared Ti Lung. He surged into the air. His tail spikes lashed out at the centipede. He hovered a moment and then, in terror, Ti Lung dove under the bridge.

Now, dragons are very brave folk, but it is true that they fear centipedes above all else.

Ying Shao ran across the river and hurried home to his bed.

The next day at dusk, Ying Shao again set out for Kal-Li's house. At the River Dragon's bridge, he set down the bowl of rice, hastily bowed, then raced across.

The banquet on his second night was more splendid than on the first. And Kal-Li had never looked lovelier than in her brocade robes and multicolored scarf. Ying Shao hardly noticed what he ate – until the main course was brought in: roasted swallows stuffed with mushrooms!

"My wife is an excellent cook, Honorable Son-to-Be," said the goldsmith. "Don't you agree?"

Ying Shao smiled and nodded. So once more he had to eat the swallows on his plate, and by the end of the meal he was worried. He opened his fortune cookie and read:

> River Dragon's greatest love:
> "Give me swallows and I shall thrive."
> River Dragon's greatest fear:
> A silk scarf of colors five.

Kal-Li was wearing a silk scarf of five colors!

As he was leaving the party, Ying Shao asked Kal-Li, "Fairest Maiden, my Bride-to-Be, give me your scarf as a token of your love."

"Yes, Husband-to-Be." She gave him the scarf, and Ying Shao tucked it into his tunic, close to his heart.

Ying Shao strode confidently toward his home. What did it matter that he had a belly full of swallows? He had a five-colored silk scarf to protect him.

As he began to cross the Jasper River, Ti Lung again flew onto the center of the bridge.

"Not-So-Honorable Sir, we meet again. Surely you have brought swallows as a gracious gift tonight," he said in a voice like the clang of a brass gong.

Ying Shao answered, "Yes, Honorable Ti Lung, I have brought you a gift."

He took the scarf out of his pocket and waved it in Ti Lung's whiskers.

"Hsi! Hsi!" thundered the River Dragon. He bolted into the air, clawing madly at the scarf. Then he dove back under the bridge.

Now, dragons are very brave folk, but it is true that they fear five-colored silk scarves almost as much as they fear centipedes.

Ying Shao raced across the bridge and did not stop shaking until he was safe in his own bed. He did not notice that the scarf had blown away in the gust of wind from the dragon's flight.

The next day at dusk, Ying Shao set out for the last banquet. At the River Dragon's bridge, he laid down a bowl of rice, bowed quickly, then sped across.

Once again the banquet was more splendid than the night before. Kal-Li's ebony hair was covered with a jeweled veil.

And again the goldsmith's wife had prepared a special swallow dish: Mandarin swallows in orange sauce. Once more Ying Shao had to smile and eat it all.

Then he confidently cracked open his fortune cookie and read:

> River Dragon's greatest love:
> The mother pearl of dragon lore.
> River Dragon's greatest fears:
> Scarf, centipede, and nothing more.

The fortune was no help this time. Ying Shao reached into his tunic for the scarf, but it wasn't there. Now he began to worry.

After the banquet, Ying Shao slowly walked home. With downcast eyes, he searched for centipedes, but he saw none.

The moon lit his way. As he reached the bridge, he gazed into the Jasper River at the moon's reflection.

"Oh, fair Chiang-O, beautiful Lunar Queen, help me!" he cried.

Just then Ti Lung flowed out from under the bridge.

His voice rang like a hammer on an iron anvil. "Dishonorable Sir, you will not escape me this time. Now give me the swallows!"

"Wait!" cried Ying Shao. "You want only swallows when I have brought you a more noble gift? Look there in the river, I have brought you the giant mother pearl, the Night-Shining Pearl."

Now, it is true that dragons have a good sense of smell, but they cannot *see* very well. When Ti Lung saw the moon's reflection in the river, he thought it really was a huge pearl.

Ti Lung flew into the air and dropped the pearl from his back claw. He rose high into the starry sky. Then he dove for the Night-Shining Pearl.

Never in his life had Ying Shao heard such an uproar. Clanging scales, spurting water, a rumbling as the bedrock of the river bed cracked, and then silence.

Ying Shao opened his eyes. Ti Lung was dead, his body slowly drifting downstream. He stumbled over something in the middle of the bridge—it was Ti-Lung's pearl.

Ying Shao and Kal-Li were married soon afterward, and they lived well for many years on the wealth from the River Dragon's pearl. But when the spring rains come and the current flows deep in the Jasper River, Ying Shao still remembers. During each spring storm he listens and wonders about the smooth river pebbles. The thunder, the rumble, are they only a spring storm? Or are they a cracking, a hatching of a river stone, a dragon leaping into the sky with a roar?